Beyond

Meet the mysterious, raggedy spirit who in the shadows beyond the firelight; the fairy child who befriends a lonely young boy; the greedy boggart, and the three strange spinners . . .

Here are four beautifully illustrated stories of goblins and other magical creatures, based on traditional folk and fairy tales.

They are ideal for reading aloud, or for children of six and up to read to themselves.

Other collections of stories in
Young Piper include:

Fog Hounds, Wind Cat, Sea Mice
Joan Aiken

It Shouldn't Happen to a Frog
Catherine Storr

The Worm and the Toffee-Nosed Princess
Eva Ibbotson

Tales of Little Brown Mouse
Tales of Little Grey Rabbit
Foxglove Tales
Alison Uttley

Beyond the Firelight

and other stories of hobgoblins

Ann Lawrence

illustrated by
Gail Lewton

PIPER BOOKS
in association with Macmillan

First published 1983 in the *Flying Carpets* series by
Macmillan Children's Books
This Piper edition published 1988 by Pan Books Ltd.
Cavaye Place, London SW10 9PG
9 8 7 6 5 4 3 2 1

ISBN 0 330 29499 7

Phototypeset by Input Typesetting Ltd, London

Printed and bound in Great Britain by
Richard Clay Limited, Bungay, Suffolk

Contents

Beyond the Firelight

There was once a rich farmer who had the worst luck in the world. One after another, he lost his money, his land and then his wife. For a time he kept going with the little he had left – a fishing boat, a tiny cottage and just enough land to support a cow, a couple of pigs and a few hens – but soon he too died, when his son was still hardly more than a boy.

Luckily, young Will had relatives and friends, who all wanted to do their best for him, They reckoned that the sale of the cottage and land should raise enough money to pay for Will to learn a trade, and since his uncle in the nearby town was willing to give him a home, everything seemed to be nicely settled.

Except that Will had other ideas. He wanted to stay where he was, living off his cow, his pigs, his fowls and his fishing, as his father had.

"What was enough for two of us, should be enough for one," he said. "Why should I work for someone else all my life, when I could be my own master?"

In short, he refused to move.

First his relatives argued, then they scolded him for being obstinate and ungrateful, but at last his father's oldest friend said:

"Why not let the boy try his luck? The chances are he'll soon find he's bitten off more than he can chew, then he may be glad to take up our suggestions."

In the end they followed his advice. Off they all went wagging their heads and telling each other that it would be only a matter of weeks before Will came round to beg their pardons.

They were right – and they were wrong.

Will did soon find he had bitten off more than he could chew, but chew it he would, though it choke him. He made up his mind to starve, before he would give up.

It was bitter hard work, all the same, and all the harder because there was no one to share it, and no one to say 'Well done!' when it was finished. He worked from dawn to dusk, just to scratch a living. His clothes fell in tatters, and the cottage became dirty and uncomfortable, because he had no time to do more than keep himself and his few animals fed. More than once he came near to giving in: more than once a day, if the truth were told. The day when he thought he had made the catch of a life-time, only to find his net full of seaweed and drift-

wood, was a day like that. By the time he had rowed back to the beach, he was too tired to sort out the mess of net and weed, and so he left it in a nasty heap at the bottom of the boat. That night he kicked off his boots and fell asleep on his bed fully dressed.

The cottage was nothing but one large room, with the bed at one end, a table and chairs at the other, and the big fireplace in the middle. The fire was low and the kettle cold when Will came home, but he could not be bothered to do anything about either.

In the early hours of the morning, however, he woke to the flicker of firelight. Propping himself up on one elbow, he saw that the fire had burned up in a big cheerful blaze. He blinked sleepily, comforted but puzzled. Suddenly his eye was drawn by a movement just beyond the firelight. As he sat up, a strange figure shuffled to the hearth.

Will could not tell exactly how tall the creature might be, for it crouched in front of the fire like a dog, its long hands resting on the floor between its huge feet. Its head was large too, and the face lit up by the restless flames was like a crumpled leather bag. Yet its body seemed small and its limbs thin. Probably it would be much shorter than a man if it stood upright, thought Will. It appeared to be dressed in seaweed, unless the ragged strips of brown stuff which covered it were actually growing on it like hair. Then the creature turned and looked towards the bed. Its expression was sad and not at all alarming, but all at once Will's curiosity turned to panic.

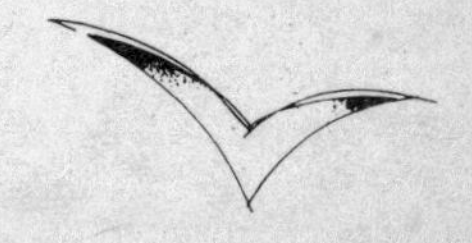

"Evil spirit be gone in God's name!" he gabbled. Remembering that unearthly things were supposed to fear iron, he grabbed his candlestick from the chest beside his bed and threw it.

His strange visitor moved then, sure enough, though it did not vanish in a puff of smoke, but simply shuffled back into the shadows with a hurt look, as anyone might, who had a candlestick thrown at him!

When Will woke next morning at sunrise, he thought he must have been dreaming. But there was the fire burning brightly, there was the kettle already boiling for his tea, and there was

his candlestick lying in front of the hearth, which had been swept clean. Nevertheless, it was only when he went down to his boat, that he was forced to believe in what he had seen. For the tangle of weed he had fished up had gone, and the net lay neatly folded. It had even been repaired.

From then on the cottage was always clean, the fire always alight. Will's clothes were quietly washed and mended overnight, and one morning, when he overslept, he found the cow had been milked and the eggs collected as well. He seldom saw his helper after that first night, but he had a feeling that he was no longer alone.

Now that he did not have to worry about keeping house, Will could turn all his energy to farming and fishing. He was a hard-working lad, and things went well for him, so that before long people stopped wondering when he would give up. Soon it was being said that Will's luck was as good as his father's had been bad. Knowing neighbours told each other that he was bound to get on in the world, though they were probably the same knowing folk, who had said just the opposite not twelve months before!

In the spring of the following year Will found time to go to church more often than he had lately, and somehow he always seemed to walk home with the same bright-faced girl. She was the daughter of the neighbour, who had advised Will's family to let him go his own way, and seeing how well the lad was making out, the good farmer had no reason to regret his words.

Will became busier than ever. He built another room on the cottage. He rented more land from his friendly neighbour and bought more animals. And in due course he asked Joan to marry him.

Naturally Joan took a great interest in her future home.

"A sad muddle it must be," she said happily. "Men can never look after themselves."

She was very surprised to find the cottage as clean and neat as a new pin. She marvelled how Will found time to do everything. Bad Will smiled modestly and said: "Oh, there's always time, if you organize things properly."

Joan was a little put out. She hoped she would be able to organize the housework so well when she took over.

However, she soon found work enough to satisfy her, for though clean, the place was bare of comforts. She sewed tirelessly to make curtains, cushions, tablecloths and sheets, and she was delighted to see how cheerful the litle house looked, when she had smartened it up.

At last they were married. The first morning after Will brought her home, Joan rose early and tied on her apron, ready to prove herself as good a housekeeper as Will. But the floors were swept and the fire was made already.

That night after supper Will said:

"Leave the dishes for now."

And it was not until next morning that she remembered them. By then, they had been done.

When, on the third morning, she found that all their clothes had been washed and ironed and were airing in front of the fire, Joan decided the joke had gone far enough.

"Will, you've shown me how well you keep house," she said. "Now leave it to me."

"Why worry?" said Will airily.

But Joan would not be put off.

"Because it's my job now," she insisted.

Then Will looked uneasy.

"Ah. Well. Yes," he said, and then: "Oh, all right. I'll show you tonight. Then you'll understand."

And though Joan was bursting with curiosity, he would not say another word about it.

That night, as the clock struck midnight, Will woke Joan and, finger on lips, he opened the bedroom door a crack, so that she could peep into the living room and see the housekeeper at work.

He had not changed in the years since Will had first seen him, except that he looked happier.

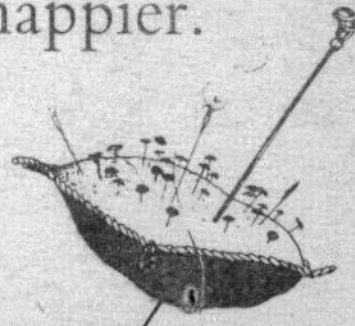

Indeed, he pursed his lips as he went about his work, as if he were whistling, although they could hear no sound. Will closed the door softly.

"There," he said. "And he's quite harmless – even has salt in his porridge; nothing wicked could stand that."

Joan did not know what to say at first. To have a servant was very fine, but such a one! Then again, she was glad to find that Will was not so clever after all, but she was less pleased about the way he had let her believe he was. Still, in the end she had to agree that it was a very handy arrangement.

All the same, she could not take Will's housekeeper as much for granted as he did. She wondered how happy it was really, and always added a good splash of cream to the porridge Will left on the hearth each night. One day she said, "Will, I don't think we do enough for him."

"Who?" said Will.

"Him. Who does the work."

"We feed him," said Will. "What else can we do?"

"Well, what about clothes?" said Joan. "He's only got those weedy rags – if they are clothes at all."

"That's the way he is." Will looked doubtful. "I think you should leave well alone."

But Joan had an idea. One night a few weeks later she laid a small pair of seaman's trousers and a good jersey (all of her own making) next to the plate on the hearth. They waited at the bedroom door, to see what the creature would make of her gift.

At first he did not seem to realize that the clothes were for him. He patted them, he fingered them, he seemed to be trying to remember something. Then he held the jersey against himself and turned towards the bedroom door.

Joan was amazed to see enormous tears rolling down the leathery cheeks. Slowly he dressed, all the time shaking his head and muttering soundlessly, then with one last look at the bedroom he shuffled out.

"There" said Will. "Now you'll have to do the housework, whether you like it or not."

"What?" Joan stared at him. "Why?"

"Because you've just paid off our housekeeper. According to the stories, if you give clothes to a house fairy, it goes away."

"Fairy? That?" Joan exclaimed.

"He must be something of that sort," said Will. "Poor old thing! He probably thought you wanted to get rid of him."

Joan was very upset.

"He mustn't think that!" she cried. She thought hard for a minute. "Perhaps giving clothes doesn't get rid of things like him – perhaps it sets them free. Perhaps he had to serve you, when you caught him like that. He might be sorry to leave us, but still be glad to be free."

"He always seemed happy enough," said Will, but he was a shade uneasy. "Anyway, he's gone now. You should have left things alone, as I said."

"I wonder what he was really," said Joan.

Will was right. Whatever the reasons for the creature's long service, Joan's gift ended it. But though the fire was no longer tended, nor the housework done quietly in the night, the good luck stayed with them. Indeed, sometimes when she was alone in the house, Joan was not sure that he really had gone altogether. Something kindly seemed to come and go; maybe visiting as a friend, she thought, now that he was no longer bound as a servant.

Only Me

John lived with his grandmother in a cottage by the sea. There were two rooms in the cottage: a large living room and a small bedroom, where Grandmother slept in her four-poster bed with red curtains. John's little bed with the patchwork quilt was in a corner of the living room.

Sometimes when Grandmother put him to bed, she told him stories about the patches.

"This was my grandma's wedding dress," she would say. "This was my father's best waistcoat: it was white silk embroidered with scarlet poppies and blue cornflowers . . . I wore this at my first dance . . . This was your mother's best dress when she was your age . . ."

Grandmother showed John a hundred years of family history in his quilt.

John did not go to school. He did his lessons with his grandmother every morning, and every afternoon he helped her in the house and garden. Sometimes they went to the beach to collect driftwood for the fire. Then when Grandmother rested in the shelter of a breakwater, John marched along the sands with a stick on his shoulder, imagining a line of red-coated soldiers marching behind him. In the evenings Grandmother sat spinning and telling old stories. In summer she sat at the cottage door, in winter she sat beside the fire.

On winter nights the noise of the wind and sea often kept John awake. Then he crept out of bed again, poked up the fire and sat in front of it, wrapped in his quilt, making his own stories about the pictures he saw in the flames.

One stormy night when John was watching the fire, there came a great gust of wind, that pulled the flames up the chimney. He heard a slithering in the flue. A shower of soot rattled down, and one enormous lump bounced out on the hearthrug. John was about to sweep it up, when it shook itself, wriggled and straightened

up, shaking soot all over the rug. There stood a tiny person, less than half as big as John: a tiny, grubby person in a green tunic.

"Hallo," said John. "Who are you?"

"Ha!" said the small person. She started to dance, scattering soot everywhere and singing.

"My name is Hob and Lob and Nixie,
Robin, Roundcap, Puck and Pixie,
Goodfellow, Brownie, Snip-snap-snorum,
Airy-fairy, High-cockalorum!"

"Is *all* that your name?" said John in amazement.

"That's only part of it," said the fairy, jumping on the hearthstone. "What's yours?"

John was ashamed of having such a short name.

"Oh, I'm only me," he mumbled.

"Onlyme," said the fairy. "That's a funny name." She started dancing again. "Onlyme, Onlyme," she sang. Everywhere she stepped, she scattered sooty smuts.

"You're making everything dirty," said John.

"So what?" said the fairy, treading soot all over the floor. "I'll do what I like!"

"But I'll get the blame for it." said John.

The fairy looked at him.

"Oh," she said. "All right." She sat on the hearth facing him. "What shall we play?" Before John could answer she jumped up again. "I know!" She grabbed a handful of cinders. "We'll play this."

She tossed the cinders and tried to catch them on the back of her hand. They all fell off.

"That's Five Stones." said John.

He showed her how to throw and catch the pieces, but she could not do it as well as he did.

"It's a silly game!" she said. She snatched the cinders from him and threw them into the fire.

"All right," said John. 'We'll do something else.'

He fetched some wool from Grandmother's work-basket and showed the fairy how to make the cat's cradle.

"I can do it! I can do it!" cried the fairy eagerly. But when she tried, she made such a tangle that she tied her own hands together.

"That's another silly game!" she said, when John had untangled her. "Don't you know anything sensible?"

Just then there came a loud whistling in the chimney. The fairy looked up.

"It's my mother," she said, and jumped up the flue, without even saying goodbye.

John swept up the mess as well as he could, but in the morning Grandmother said: "There was quite a storm last night. Just look at the soot it brought down!"

John said nothing. He never told tales.

That afternoon John and his grandmother went to the seashore. When they had all the wood they could carry, Grandmother sat down, while John skimmed pebbles over the waves. Suddenly he heard a tiny voice call:

"Onlyme! What are you doing?"

It was the fairy child, dancing towards him along the beach.

"Playing ducks and drakes," he said.

"I can do that," she said, picking up a pebble. But it was the wrong shape, and she threw it the wrong way, so instead of skipping over the water like the one John had thrown, it went plop – straight in!

"It's a silly game!" she said crossly, knocking John's pebbles out of his hand. "I can duck and drake myself." She bounced into the air, drew her knees up to her chin and bounced out to sea. Then she turned and danced on the spray, waving to John.

"And I can ride the sea horses!" she shouted.

John did not understand what she meant, but then he saw that the waves were full of little white horses, all galloping to the beach, though he could not see where they went, when they reached it. The fairy rode in on their backs.

"There." She said, landing beside him again. "Now what shall we do?"

"We could play soldiers," said John. To his surprise she was eager to play. The trouble was, she wanted to change everything. First she wanted to be the French, then she wanted the French to win.

"But they didn't win," said John reasonably. The fairy threw down her stick.

"It's a silly game," she said. "I'm going." And she danced away down the beach, in and out of the spray.

John was too sleepy that night to watch the fire. In fact he was almost asleep when he heard someone call: "Onlyme!"

He opened his eyes. The fairy child was standing on the hearth, looking round for him.

"Oh, there you are," she said when he sat up. "What shall we play?"

Since she tired of every game so quickly, John wondered why she still wanted to play with him.

"Can you play draughts?" he asked, because it was the first thing that came into his head.

"No, but you can teach me," said the fairy.

Of course, she had hardly learnt the rules before she was bored again.

"This is dull," she complained. "Haven't you got anything else?" She ran to the cupboard and jumped right inside. In a moment he heard her squeak with excitement. "I've found little men!" She jumped out with a chess piece in each hand. "What game is this?"

"It's chess," said John. "I don't know how to play it, but Grandma says it's like a battle."

"A battle!" said the fairy. "What fun! I'll show you this one!"

She stood all the chessmen on the hearthrug, and snapped her fingers. To John's amazement the two sides shuffled into lines facing each other and marched together. The fairy laughed and

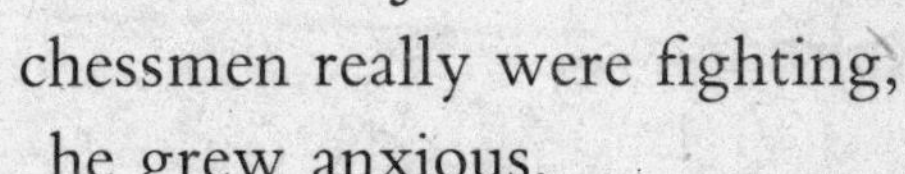

clapped but when John saw that the chessmen really were fighting, he grew anxious.

"They might get broken," he said nervously.

"That's what happens in a battle," said the fairy.

"They mustn't!" said John, because he knew they were old and valuable. "Stop them!"

"Shan't!" said the fairy. It looked as if the chessmen jostled together harder.

"Stop them!" John shouted, slapping the fairy's arm.

At once the chessmen were still, but the fairy set up such a roar that John was sure his grandmother would hear. He jumped into bed and pulled the covers over his head, leaving the fairy howling on the hearthrug. Once again he heard the whistling in the chimney, but this time he heard a voice too.

"What's the matter?" it called. "Is someone hurting you?"

"Yes!" wailed the fairy

There was a swish in the flue and a soft patter on the hearth.

"Who?" the voice demanded, right in the room. John peeped out and saw another, bigger fairy standing on the hearthstone. She looked very fierce.

"It was Onlyme," cried the fairy child.

"What?" her mother exclaimed. "If it was only you, you've nothing to complain about, have you?" With that she seized her child and threw her up the chimney.

John ducked under the covers again, not at all wanting to be noticed by the angry mother. He kept still for a long time, before he poked his head out and sat up. The fairy mother was sitting on the end of his bed.

"Oh," said John.

"Don't be afraid," said the fairy. "It's only me."

"Oh," said John again. "I'm sorry . . ."

The fairy shrugged.

"I expect she was asking for it." She seemed to be more interested in the patchwork quilt than in her child's quarrels. She pointed to one of the patches. "I knew the girl who wore that," she went on. It was Great-great-grandma's wedding dress.

"But that was nearly a hundred years ago," John said, staring.

"That's nothing," said the fairy. "Do you know what that was?" She prodded another patch with her thin finger, a patch embroidered with a curly leaf and flower.

"That's from curtains Great-great-grandpa's mother gave to Great-great-grandma," John told her.

"Oh, but they were a hundred years older than that," said the fairy. "I used to gossip with the girl who made them, while she worked. We were both young then, Jane and I." She sighed. "And now my own child plays with Jane's umpteen times great-grandson."

"Can she still play with me?" John asked timidly.

"Do you still want her to?" the fairy demanded, fixing her sharp eyes on him again.

"Well, there isn't anyone else," he said.

"Humph!" The fairy frowned. "It's just only you, is it?"

John nodded.

"All right." The fairy jumped down and ran to the fireplace. "You shall have someone to play with. I don't say it'll be my bad child – but I don't say it won't be either."

With a hop and a spring she disappeared up the chimney. The fire burst into flames that leapt up as if to follow her.

John did not see the fairy child again. He did his lessons alone and played alone as before. But

one morning when Grandma woke him, she put a little wriggling thing on the bed beside him. It was a white puppy with reddish-brown ears.

"It's one of Bess's puppies, from the farm," she said. "Mrs Ellis thought she'd be company for you."

"I'll call her Pixie," said John, holding up the puppy. "Airy-fairy-tricksie-pixie!"

"That's a big name for a small beast!" Grandmother exclaimed. "But you could be right – fairy dogs were always white with red ears in the old tales."

The puppy squirmed and tried to chew John's thumb.

"I expect she's very bad," said John, pretending to frown.

"I hope not!" said Grandmother.

But she was.

She ran dirty footprints all over the house. She pulled wool out of Grandmother's work-basket and made terrible tangles. She chewed one of the chessmen. But she played all John's games with him too, and watched the fire with him at night. And sometimes when they played on the beach, she ran into the edge of the sea, barking, until John thought he could see little white horses rearing away from her in the spray.

The Boggart

When the children took the boggart home with them they had no idea how much trouble they were bringing to the farm. One gloomy winter afternoon when they were walking home from school, a small black dog bounded out of the woods, all ready for a game. It was a bit rough but very friendly, and they played with it all the way to the farm gate. Janet even wanted to take it home, but Colin knew their mother would not let them keep it, and so they left the little animal sitting by the gate, watching them.

Later, their father, coming home for his tea, found a black calf wandering in the lane. Because it was dark by then, he did not notice that all his calves were penned already, and so he drove it into the farmyard with the others.

Early next morning Mrs Reynolds, hurrying out to collect the eggs, saw her big, black cooking-pot (as she thought) standing in the corner of the calf pen.

"How in the world did that get there?" she said to herself, and hastily returned it to the kitchen, before attending to the hens. Leaving it just inside the door, she did not notice that her own pot was still in its usual place.

And the boggart had arrived.

He started to upset things at once. The house was suddenly full of draughts, there was a peculiar smell in the cellar, and things were forever falling over without anyone touching them.

"I don't know what's wrong," said Mrs Reynolds. "I can't seem to get warm, and the chimney's smoking something awful."

"Wind's gone round," said her husband.

She sniffed.

"I'm sure we never had that smell before, whichever way the wind blew."

Soon it became quite plain that the trouble had nothing to do with the weather.

The bread did not rise, the milk curdled, the fire was always going out. The cat would suddenly leap up and run out, as if someone had kicked her. The children's porridge was spilt, their clothes torn, their toys thrown about. Then the furniture started to shift around of its own accord; pots and pans hurtled across the kitchen without warning, and even Mr Reynolds had to admit that something very odd and rather nasty was going on.

"We've got a boggart," he said. "That's the only thing I can think of that acts like this. I've heard tell of them, but I never really believed in that sort of thing till now."

The children were rather proud of their invisible lodger, in spite of the trouble he caused, but their father shook his head.

"I don't know how we let him in (because he couldn't have got in without our help), but we could be stuck with him now for good. And it could get worse."

It did. The smell spread to fill the whole house, and they were forever dodging the things the boggart threw at them. The children still found this amusing, and made up a mad

catching game with him. Their parents were not amused at all, and at last they could stand it no longer. A mile or so away there was an empty cottage that belonged to the farm, and though it was small, they decided to move there.

"The old devil won't leave us, so we'll have to leave him," the farmer declared. "Only he mustn't guess, or he'll find some way of coming with us."

They made their plans secretly, then early one morning they piled all the household gear into a cart and left the farm on tiptoe. At the bottom of the lane they met their nearest neighbour, driving to market in her pony and trap. She was surprised, as well she might be, for the Reynolds

family had never done anything at all unusual in a hundred years.

"What's this then?" she exclaimed.

The farmer and his wife felt rather foolish to be caught like this, but the children, thinking they were now far enough on their way, were eager to explain. Only before any of them could speak, a voice came hollowly from the back of the cart.

"Sssh!" it whispered loudly. "Don't tell anyone – we're flitting!"

Everyone turned in time to see the lid of a

chest lowering itself. They all stared. Then Mr Reynolds grunted and turned the cart round.

"If you're flitting with us, we might as well flit back!" he said.

And they headed back to the farm, leaving the astonished lady gazing open-mouthed after them.

Having once spoken, the boggart became tiresomely noisy, whistling out of tune and breaking into conversations in the rudest manner. Next he allowed himself to be seen. First he was only a wavering, smoky outline; then they saw bits of him – the hand that threw the plate, the foot that kicked the cat. Finally he became completely visible: an ugly, malicious little goblin. Yet even then he did not seem altogether solid. By that time he had made himself so much at home, that you might have thought *he* owned the place. Indeed, it seemed that he thought that himself, for as the winter drew to an end, he started scheming to settle himself on the farm for life (and a boggart's life is very, very, long!).

One morning in early spring, when the family were sitting at breakfast in the big farmhouse kitchen, the boggart pushed Colin off his stool and appeared on it himself, elbows on the table and grinning unpleasantly.

"Lookee here, master," he said to Mr Reynolds. "I got an idea. Sharing quarters like this ain't convenient for any of us, so what say I set meself up in the barn?"

The family looked at each other, hardly daring to believe their luck.

"Mind you," the boggart went on cunningly. "I'd want something to make up for the trouble of moving out."

"What?" said Mr Reynolds.

"Fair's fair." The boggart grinned even wider. "Reckon a half-share in the crop of that big field would do me. Say, I take everything above the ground and you have everything below."

Mr Reynolds thought a minute, his face very solemn.

"All right, bogie," he said at last. "That's what we'll do."

That very day the boggart moved out of the house, and Mr Reynolds set the big field with potatoes.

When he saw the plants growing up well and the fruit forming, the boggart thought the crop was tomatoes (because tomato and potato plants look very much alike at first). He reckoned he was going to do well out of his bargain. You can imagine his fury a month or two later, when he discovered that the real crop was below the ground, and that his share was worthless. All the same, since he had proposed the plan himself, he was bound to keep his word, and for a full year the family lived in their own home in peace. The following spring he was determined not to be caught out again. A year to the day after his first attempt he appeared again at the breakfast table.

"Fair's fair," he said, still grinning, but maybe not so widely now. "We'll have it t'other way round this year."

"Just what I was going to suggest myself," said Mr Reynolds.

That year he sowed the field with wheat.

The boggart was livid with rage. If anyone went near the barn, he hurled things and yelled horribly, but he still had to stay out of the house, and everyone thought it was worth losing the use of the barn for the sake of that. Nevertheless, when the third spring came he popped up in the kitchen as before, ready to bargain again with his "partner", as he called Mr Reynolds. This time the farmer put his word in first.

"I'll tell you right away what I'm doing with that field this year," he said. "I'm putting it down to grass. And we won't have any fiddle-faddle about sharing: we'll have a little competition for it. Come haymaking, you mow one half of it and I'll mow t'other. Whichever finishes first, wins the field outright."

At that, the boggart's grin returned as broad as ever. He knew what he could do, when he had a mind, and he was sure the field was as good as his. He reckoned too, that if he could win the field, he could win the whole farm in the end.

A little while before haymaking that year, Mr Reynolds went into the village to see the blacksmith, who came up to the farm a few days later with some machinery he had been repairing for the farmer. In the bottom of his cart he also had a lot of something else wrapped in sacking, but neither he nor Mr Reynolds had anything to say about this part of his load, which had vanished mysteriously by the time he went back to his forge.

The night before the mowing contest Mrs Reynolds and the children were anxious and excited, but the farmer was as calm as ever, and went out for a walk by himself. He was gone a long time.

The next day dawned fine and perfect for mowing. Nearly bursting with conceit, the boggart took his place on one side of the field. Mr Reynolds waited quietly on the other. When the signal was given, they both began to mow with steadily swinging scythes. Presently, however, it seemed as if the boggart was in

trouble. The rhythm of his swing was broken, and he started muttering to himself:

"Dang these thistles! Drat these tarnation burdocks!"

After an hour he had fallen well behind Mr Reynolds and was slowing down even more.

"Hey, master!" he shouted. "When do we wiffle-waffle?" (meaning when could they sharpen their scythes, which contestants in a mowing competition had to do at the same time).

The farmer felt the edge of his scythe.

"'Bout noon, I reckon."

The boggart groaned and went on mowing. Another hour later he stopped again.

"'Ain't it noon yet?" he demanded, eyeing his scythe glumly. "This blade o' mine's as round as a bear's behind!"

The farmer looked at the sun, then fished his big watch out of his waistcoat pocket.

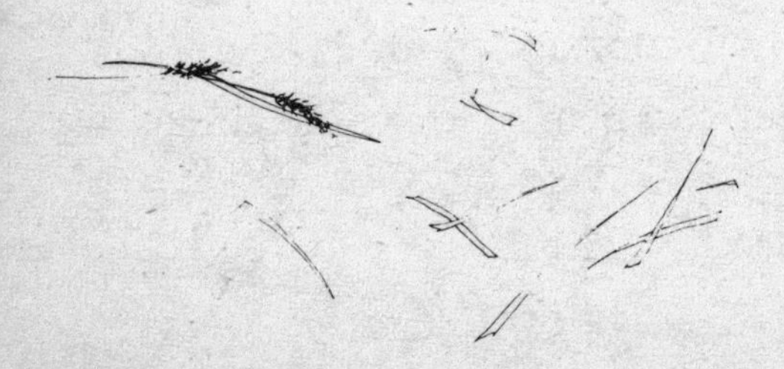

"'Nother couple of hours," he said calmly.

The boggart looked round the field: Mr Reynolds had already mown twice as much as he had. He threw down his scythe.

"Tarnation field!" he yelled. He jumped on the scythe and broke it in pieces. "Tarnation farm!" He picked up the pieces and threw them violently into the hedge. "Dang it!" With a shriek of rage he vanished, never to be seen again.

Mr Reynolds' family and friends who had come to watch the competition, gathered round to congratulate him.

"Well John," said one of his neighbours. "I was sure that old bogie would win – he was going like a train at the start. What happened to him?"

The farmer laughed.

"Ah, but there was more than grass sown on that half of the field," he said. He walked across and parted the unmown grass on the boggart's side to show them dozens of thin steel rods stuck in the ground. Then he looked at the part the boggart had managed to mow and laughed even more. "Well look at that!" he said, when he recovered. "The old devil mowed clean through every one he came to! If he could have waffled when he wanted to, I reckon he might have beaten me in spite of them!"

The Three Spinners

Meg was a good girl, kind, sweet tempered and neat, yet she drove her poor mother nearly mad. Mrs Lindsey was a widow, who made her living by spinning. She worked fast, made good yarn of every sort, and if only Meg could have done half as well, they might have been quite comfortable. Not that Meg was lazy, in fact she was painfully hardworking – but so slow! Her carding was beautiful, but it took her all day to card as much wool as her mother could spin in an hour. The thread she spun was firm and even, but she rarely did more than half a skein a day. Her mother did not know what to do with her.

"You must have been born to be a lady, my girl," she would cry. "For you'll never make your own living!"

And Meg would hang her head, blushing, and never say a word.

One evening when Mrs Lindsey was scolding her daughter like this, because she had done so little that day, the lady of the manor called to collect some yarn, and overheard part of what was said.

My Lady was the old squire's widow. She had run his estates ever since he had died, and though her son was now old enough to take over, she still had a finger in every local pie, and her nose in everyone's business.

"What's this?" she exclaimed, bustling into the cottage with only a tap at the door. "Trouble? What's wrong with little Meg's spinning, then?"

Poor Mrs Lindsey was terribly flustered, and so she pretended to laugh, and said: "Dear me, there's nothing wrong with it at all! Look how fine it is. But she's so fond of spinning, she won't leave her wheel to do anything else." She waved recklessly towards a great basket of yarn. "She did all that only today!"

My Lady's eyes widened.

"All that? Why there must be the best part of a whole fleece there!" For a moment she stood tapping her leg with her riding crop and thinking, then she added: "I could do with a girl who loves spinning that much. Our sheep

have just been shorn, and I've got a whole roomful of fleece."

Horrified, Mrs Lindsey began to protest, but Madam raised one hand.

"Neither of you shall lose by the arrangement. If she's as good as you say, I'll pay her well." She turned to leave. "Send her up to the Hall tomorrow."

It seemed to Meg and her mother as if they had no choice. Next morning the girl went meekly to the Hall, and was taken to a room stacked to the ceiling with fleeces.

"A fleece a day," said My Lady. "At that rate you should be finished by harvest. I'll have a bed put in here for you, so that you don't have to waste a moment."

At first Meg really tried to spin as fast as she could. She sat at her wheel day and night, until she was so tired she could have cried, but after a few days she saw that she could never spin all that wool by harvest time. She knew no one could do it.

Mrs Lindsey had hoped she might be able to help, but My Lady kept such a close watch on Meg that nobody could slip into the spinning room unseen, or smuggle any fleece out. Madam was as sure as Meg that the task was impossible, but she meant to show up her mother's silly boasting.

So Meg sat alone, day after day, spinning slowly and carefully, while the huge pile of fleeces never seemed to get any smaller. Her only friend was the young squire, who had looked in one day out of curiosity, and finding Meg's quiet voice as soothing as the whirr of her spinning wheel, he had fallen into the habit of sitting with her most afternoons. Sometimes he coaxed her to walk with him in the summer evenings, and as the time ran out, Meg became more willing to be persuaded.

Of course the young man's mother knew all about these walks and talks, and they did not please her. She even suspected Mrs Lindsey of making her boast with the idea of drawing the squire's attention to her daughter. One afternoon Madam visited Meg's room. She frowned at her son, then cast an eye over the great sack of unspun fleeces and the very small pile of finished skeins.

"My word child!" she exclaimed. "You must be an even quicker worker than your mother said, if you can leave all that to the last minute!"

The spinning was to be finished by the day of the harvest supper. On the very last day Meg was too miserable and fearful to leave her room, or to let her friend come in, though she did even less spinning than usual. By nightfall she had stopped altogether, unable to see for crying.

The door clicked, and footsteps came towards her, tip-tap, tip-tap across the bare boards. Meg looked up, then started with surprise. The strangest little woman stood before her. She was no more than three feet tall and wore funny old-fashioned clothes. But the oddest thing about her was her feet, for her right foot was twice the size of the left.

"What's to do?" she demanded.

Meg, speechless with tears and amazement, pointed hopelessly at the fleeces and the wheel.

"Is that all?" said the old woman. "Nothing there to cry about. Lie down and sleep. It'll all be done by morning."

Meg tried to thank her (even though she did not believe a word she said), but the old woman shook her head briskly.

"No need for thanks. I only want one thing – an invitation to your wedding."

"I shall never marry," said Meg, finding her voice at last, for she was sure the only person she wanted to marry would never want to marry her.

"We'll see," said the old woman. "Go to sleep,"

Which was exactly what Meg did the moment her head touched the pillow. She slept until My Lady came to wake her, and they both stared at the bales of spun skeins, which were piled in place of the raw fleeces.

My Lady was amazed, Meg's mother could not believe her eyes, but the young squire had no trouble believing it at all. It simply proved to him that Meg was the cleverest girl in the world, as well as the sweetest and prettiest.

However, it did not take My Lady long to recover. She could not believe that Meg had done the work herself, and was determined to test her again. If she really was such a wonderful spinner, well and good. Madam meant to make use of her skill. But if some trick had been played, she was going to get to the bottom of

it. A few days after the harvest supper, she came knocking at Mrs Lindsey's door, to say she hoped Meg was well rested, because the Hall could not do without her. Indeed, knowing how she loved spinning, they had bought some flax to tempt her back. Mrs Lindsey did not want her daughter to risk her luck too far, but Meg went back at once.

When she saw her spinning room piled high with flax, she almost laughed.

"I should think you might finish that by Christmas," said My Lady.

"I'll try, Ma'am." said Meg, knowing she could not do a tenth of it, but only thinking of the time she would be able to spend with My Lady's son.

That autumn My Lady began to complain that she was feeling her age, and to say that her son ought to be busier about his own affairs. She found work to occupy him all day, and often sent him away on business. But he still found time to spend with Meg. The girl was even more closely watched than she had been in the summer, and as Christmas drew near, My

Lady was sure she could not succeed this time.

The flax was to be spun by Christmas Eve, and the night before that Meg shut herself up alone again. This time she did not cry. By taking on another impossible job, she had won a few months with the young squire, and she did not see how she could ask for anything more. She

was sitting dreaming by her wheel, when the door clicked and footsteps came tip-tap, tip-tap towards her. It was the little old woman again.

But no, it was not the same little old woman, though this one was so like the first, that they must have been sisters, only instead of a huge right foot, this one had an enormous, drooping lower lip.

"Well then," said the old woman. "Same again, is it? A little bit of spinning for an invitation to your wedding?"

Meg shook her head sadly, but she could not help smiling as well.

"You'll wait a long time for that, I'm afraid,"

"We'll see," said the old woman. "Go to sleep."

And of course, when My Lady and her son came in next morning, all the flax had been spun into fine linen thread.

That was the happiest Christmas of Meg's life. On Christmas Day the young squire kissed her under the mistletoe, on New Year's Eve he whispered something in her ear, and on Twelfth

Night he told his mother that he wanted to marry the sweetest, prettiest, cleverest girl in the world. After all Meg had done, it was difficult for Madam to object, though she was still sure she had been fooled somehow. At last she gave her consent on one condition – that Meg should spin a roomful of silk by Easter.

Her son saw no reason why this should be more difficult for his clever girl than the wool or the flax, and agreed without hesitation. Meg said nothing, but all at once her wedding day seemed as far away as ever.

Since she had never handled silk before, her work this time was even slower. To make things worse, her future husband was so sure she could do it easily, that he kept taking her away from her spinning to help him plan their wedding. On the last evening Meg was too nervous to sit still, but walked up and down the room, nearly frantic with anxiety. Would help come again? When the door clicked, she did not dare look round, until the tip-tap of footsteps stopped right behind her.

"No doubt about whether there'll be a wedding now, eh?" said a cheerful voice.

Meg gasped with relief. This old woman was the very image of her two sisters, except that she had huge thumbs. Meg did not know how to thank her, but she simply laughed and sat down at the wheel.

"Just an invitation to the wedding, that's all we ask," she said. "Go to bed now, and leave this to me."

After that there was nothing more My Lady could do to delay the wedding, though she did insist that they must wait until some of the silk had been woven and made into a wedding dress.

If Meg had been a silly, conceited girl, she might have been ashamed to invite such funny old bodies as her three helpers to her wedding, but such an idea never crossed her mind. Her only worry was that she did not know where to send their invitations, or even how to address them. In the end she wrote cards to Mistress Wool, Mistress Flax and Mistress Silk, and she left them lodged on the spindle of her wheel, until she could think how to deliver them. In the morning they were gone.

The wedding was a grand affair. My Lady had decided to make the best of a bad job, but that did not mean she was any happier to have Meg for her daughter-in-law, and she took every chance to mock her on the sly.

"My son," she said. "You'll never need to wear a scrap of cloth, that isn't made from yarn spun by your own wife. That'll be worth a good dowry over the years, I can tell you."

The young man agreed eagerly, not noticing how pale Meg suddenly became.

The three spinners did not appear until the feast was at its height. Among the well-dressed wedding guests they looked stranger than ever, but Meg welcomed them warmly. Ignoring her mother-in-law's scornful glances, she introduced them as her three great-aunts. The bridegroom was courtesy itself to the old women, but in the end he simply could not help asking them how they had come by their extraordinary features.

"Spinning," they said all together.

"Treadling," said the first, poking out her great foot.

"Wetting the thread," said the second, flicking her thumb against her lower lip.

"Pulling out," said the third, displaying her two thumbs.

The young man nodded thoughtfully, then looked long and hard at his pretty bride.

Later, when the couple were alone, he said uneasily:

"My darling, I don't want to start our married life by laying down the law, but there's one thing I feel I must insist on."

"What is it?" said Meg anxiously.

"Well, my angel," he went on. "I know how much you love spinning, but I can't bear to think that you might some day become deformed by it, like your dear aunts. Promise me you'll never spin again."

Meg blushed and looked at the floor.

"Why, if that's what you want, of course I never will," she said.

And of course she never did.

Joan Aiken

Fog Hounds, Wind Cat, Sea Mice £1.75

The Fog Hounds were silent, mysterious – and deadly. They belonged to the King and they roamed all over the land from dusk to dawn. No-one who had been chased by them ever lived to tell the tale. But Tad was not afraid of them. He even wanted to own one . . .

Tad's adventure is the first in this masterly collection specially written to bridge the gap between first picture books and longer stories.

Catherine Storr

It Shouldn't Happen to a Frog and other stories £1.75

Lisa was sure she could do better than the heroines of fairy tales. After all, they had made some very stupid mistakes. But when she met the frog who was supposed to turn into a prince, things didn't turn out quite as she planned. For a start, he had some really annoying habits . . .

The adventures of Lisa – a modern girl caught up in the traditional fairy tales – have been specially written to bridge the gap between first picture books and longer stories.

Joyce Dunbar

Mundo and the Weather-Child £1.95

'I hate the garden! I hate the house!
I want to go back home.'

Edmund feels a stranger in the rambling house he and his parents have moved to, but by the time winter arrives, he is utterly lost. Unable to hear, he is locked into a solitary world of silence.

But, slowly, he discovers another world in the wild garden. There he makes friends with the Weather-Child, who climbs and rides on the weather, swinging on all its changes.

It is the Weather-Child who frees him from isolation and leads him back into the real world.

Eva Ibbotson

The Worm and the Toffee-Nosed Princess £1.75

and other stories of monsters

Why did the giant, hairy worm eat the snooty princess? What happened to the silly dog who dared to annoy a Frid? And how did the three Scotsmen deal with a sheep-eating Boobrie?

Find out the answers to these and other questions in this collection of funny tales about monsters, written specially for readers who are progressing from picture books to longer stories.

John Steinbeck
The Red Pony £1.95

This is the story of a boy, Jody, who above all wanted a pony. It is the story of how he got it, and how it died.

But Jody waited, hoped and prayed for another pony. He only had one more chance . . .

This poignant tale of a boy and his love for a pony is a modern children's classic

Felix Salten
Bambi £1.99

When Bambi leaves the secret glade in which he is born, he learns the mysteries of the forest and the ways of the animals who live there. But there is one creature – strange and terrible – whom Bambi fears above all others. It is his greatest enemy – Man.

One of the most powerful and moving animal stories ever written, BAMBI is about the life of a deer – the Young Prince of the Forest – who grows up to understand the harsh realities of life in the wild.

Alison Uttley

Tales of Little Grey Rabbit £1.99

At last – the classic you've been waiting for! A loud cheer for Little Grey Rabbit and her friends Hare, Squirrel, Moldy Warp and Fuzzypeg the hedgehog. Together for the first time, four stories which tell of their exciting adventures and escapades. Introducing the enemies, Fox and Weasel and a host of endearing animal characters. A book to be treasured.

Foxglove Tales £1.95

Nowhere is Alison Uttley's magical blend of fantasy, humour and feeling for nature more apparent than in this delightful collection of twelve of her very best stories. Five of them come from her first book, *Moonshine and Magic*, and the three from her last, *Lavender Shoes*, reveal that she had lost none of her skill at the age of eighty-six! Sam Pig and Tim Rabbit, two of her most popular heroes, are represented, and there are stories from *Nine Starlight Tales* and *The Weathercock*. Altogether, a classic to treasure.

All Pan books are available at your local bookshop or newsagent, or can be ordered direct from the publisher. Indicate the number of copies required and fill in the form below.

Send to: **CS Department, Pan Books Ltd., P.O. Box 40, Basingstoke, Hants. RG21 2YT.**

or phone: 0256 469551 (Ansaphone), quoting title, author and Credit Card number.

Please enclose a remittance* to the value of the cover price plus: 60p for the first book plus 30p per copy for each additional book ordered to a maximum charge of £2.40 to cover postage and packing.

*Payment may be made in sterling by UK personal cheque, postal order, sterling draft or international money order, made payable to Pan Books Ltd.

Alternatively by Barclaycard/Access:

Card No. | | | | | | | | | | | | | | | | |

____

Signature:

Applicable only in the UK and Republic of Ireland.

While every effort is made to keep prices low, it is sometimes necessary to increase prices at short notice. Pan Books reserve the right to show on covers and charge new retail prices which may differ from those advertised in the text or elsewhere.

NAME AND ADDRESS IN BLOCK LETTERS PLEASE:

....

Name______________________________

Address______________________________

____

____

____

3/87